ASL Tales:
The Princess and the pea

Written by Alicita Rodríguez & Joseph Starr
Illustrated by Judy Hood

Created and Performed in American Sign Language by
Pinky Aiello

ASL ❀ Tales
Portland, Oregon

The Publisher, Authors, Illustrator, and ASL Artist would like to thank
Alisha Bronk, Leif Croonquist, Liz Davis, Judy Green, Helynne Hansen,
Joe Hood, Sally Mankus, Fred Sawyer, Spencer Starr, Vini Viubatti,
and especially Janis Sawyer.

First edition 2008

Library of Congress Control Number: 2008937372

ISBN 978-0-9818139-0-5

Designed by Alicita Rodríguez & Joseph Starr

Printed in China by King's Time Printing Press

Illustrations were done in acrylic on wood

ASL Tales
25 N.W. 23rd Place
Suite 6, No. 293
Portland, OR 97210

visit us at asltales.net

To Florida School for the Deaf, where I had the privilege, at the age of 14, to FINALLY see the beauty of American Sign Language. This work is dedicated to the Deaf teachers who taught me, and to the possibility of the world seeing the value of ASL so that no Deaf child will ever again be denied this amazing language.
—Pinky Aiello

Once upon a time, there was a Prince who lived in a lovely castle. The castle had a drawbridge and a moat. It had lots of towers and turrets. But the Prince was lonely. He was very small. And his kingdom very large. So he set out on a journey to find a princess.

He traveled NORTH.
But the *princess* he found did not like warm weather.

He traveled SOUTH.

But the princess he found did not speak his language.

He traveled WEST.

But the princess he found would not leave her horses.

H_e traveled EAST.

But the **princess** he found was already married.

One dark and gloomy night, a storm gathered outside the castle. Rain spattered against the windows.

Lightning flashed and thunder crashed. Even the wind howled.

The Prince heard someone knocking at the door. When he opened it, he found a princess who was all wet.

Water dripped from her hair and from the tip of her nose.

Water pooled in her pockets and inside her shoes.

The princess asked to come in and promptly made friends with the dog. That's GOOD, thought the Prince.

At dinner, the princess was very polite. She said *please* and *thank you*, which pleased the cook very much. That's GOOD, thought the Prince.

 In the library, she read a rather big book. It was as **HEAVY** as a **BRICK**. That's GOOD, thought the Prince.

The Queen noticed that the Prince liked this princess. She was his mother, after all, and mothers always know what you're thinking! So she took the Prince into the study, where she could speak to him in private.

It seems you like this princess," said the Queen.
I do. She's kind to animals," said the Prince.
That's true," said the Queen.
And she says please and thank you," said the Prince.
That's true," said the Queen.
And she can read the biggest, heaviest books," said the Prince.
True again," said the Queen.

"But does she have the hands of a Princess?"
The Prince didn't understand, so he just shrugged his
shoulders. "Everybody knows," said the Queen,
"that a Princess must have the *smallest, thinnest*
hands. Does she have *small* and *thin* hands?"
"No," said the Prince.

 "And everybody knows," said the Queen,
"that a Princess must have *teeny
tiny* feet. Does she have *teeny tiny* feet?"
"No," said the Prince.

"And everybody knows," said the Queen, "that a Princess must
have a delicate face. Does she have a delicate face?"

"I don't know," said the Prince. He didn't understand all this talk
about thin hands, and teeny feet, and delicate faces. He thought the
princess had *beautiful* hands...and *beautiful* feet...and a *lovely* face.

"But MOST of all," said the Queen,

"everybody knows that a Princess must

have a body that's as light as the air."

The Queen and the Prince prepared the princess' bed. They found the softest mattresses, and the fluffiest pillows, and the poofiest blankets. They piled them all up to the ceiling, one on top of the next.

Underneath it all, the Queen placed a single pea. "If the princess is as light as the air," said the Queen, "she'll feel the pea underneath her. She'll toss and turn and have an awful night's sleep."

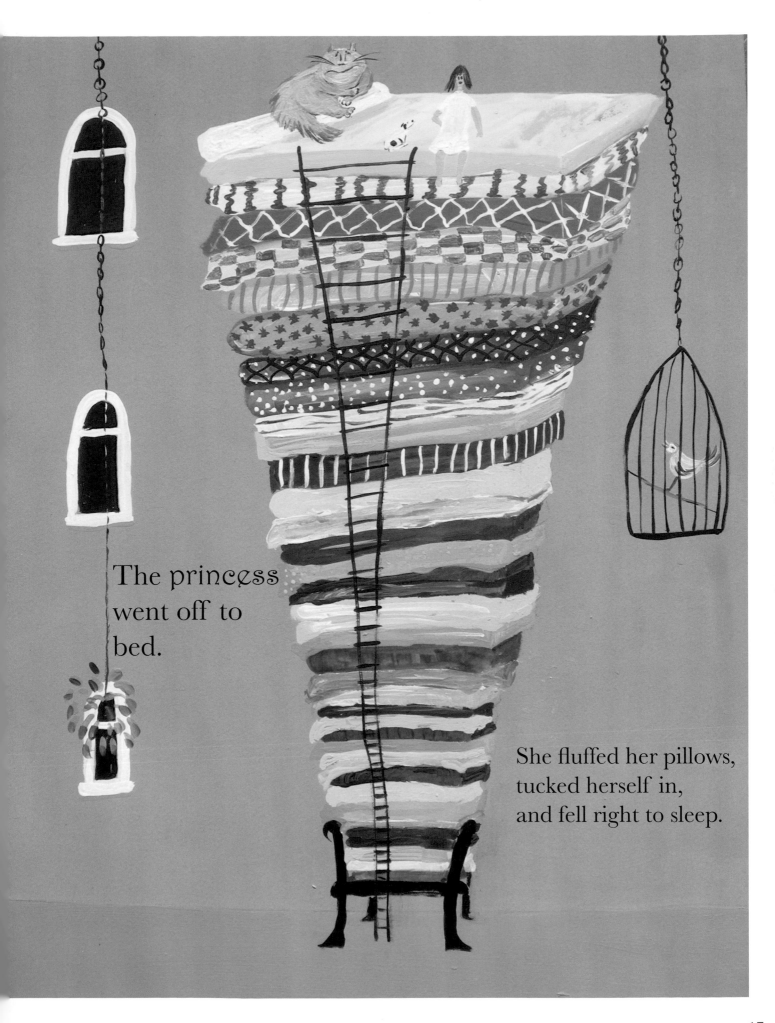

The princess
went off to
bed.

She fluffed her pillows,
tucked herself in,
and fell right to sleep.

At breakfast, the Queen and the Prince asked her how she slept. "Perfectly well," said the princess. "The pillows were lovely and the sheets were as soft as a cloud and I had such odd, enchanting dreams."

"What kinds of dreams?" asked the Prince.

"Dreams about peas," said the princess.

"First one pea fell from the sky, then two, then three. Then there was a rainstorm of peas. They filled the moat and covered the drawbridge. Everything vanished beneath so many peas, even the towers of the castle and the turrets and the stairs. And the only food in the castle was steaming hot pea soup."

The Queen didn't like all this ᴏᴏᴏꜱᴇᴏꜱᴇ about peas.

"Well, it's settled," said the Queen. "This princess does not have a body that's as light as the air. She's NOT a true Princess after all." But the Prince thought she was a *fine* princess.

That night, he put a **pea** beneath his mother's bed. When he put his ear next to her bedroom door, he heard the Queen **SNORING**. She snored quite loudly, like a roaring lion and a clucking hen.

At breakfast, the Prince asked the Queen how she slept. "Perfectly well," she said. Then the Prince held up the **pea** he had hidden beneath his mother's bed. "Well, it's settled," said the Prince. "The Queen does not have a body that's as light as the air. She's **NOT** a true queen after all." The Queen was so **SHOCKED** that she fainted, landing right in a bowl of jam.

But when she awoke, she remembered how the princess was nice and kind and intelligent, and she gave the Prince and Princess her blessing. They celebrated by going on a long, long voyage together.

They went to the frozen NORTH.

Aⁿd the sunny SOUTH.

And the wide open WEST.

They even went to the exotic EAST.

When they got back to the castle, the first thing they did was sit down to a nice, hot, steaming bowl of pea soup.

The End